The Right Moment

The Right Moment

David Belbin

A & C Black • London

WORLD WAR II FLASHBACKS

The Right Moment • David Belbin

Final Victory • Herbie Brennan

Blitz Boys • Linda Newbery

Blood and Ice • Neil Tonge

Published 2000 by A & C Black (Publishers) Ltd
35 Bedford Row, London WC1R 4JH

Text copyright © 2000 David Belbin

The right of David Belbin to be identified as author of
this work has been asserted by him in accordance
with the Copyright, Designs and Patents Act 1988.

ISBN 0-7136-5350-7

A CIP catalogue record for this book is available
from the British Library.

Printed and bound in Great Britain by
Creative Print & Design (Wales), Ebbw Vale.

For Katy Wood

Contents

Author's Note

In 1918, Germany lost the First World War. Twenty years later, the German Chancellor, Adolf Hitler, seemed determined to start a second one. International peace negotiations failed. In 1939, Germany invaded first Czechoslovakia, then Poland. On September 3rd, Britain and France declared war on Germany.

Soon, Denmark, Norway, Belgium, Holland and Luxembourg were under attack. On May 13th, the German army entered France. For each of these countries, surrender was only a matter of time.

On June 10th, just before the Germans reached Paris, the French government fled to the Loire Valley. Six days later, the French Prime Minister resigned. He was replaced by Marshal Petain, a First World War hero who was prepared to collaborate with the Germans. On June 24th, Petain signed an armistice with Germany. France was divided into two zones: the Occupied Zone (including Paris, Jean's home in the story which follows) and the Southern Zone (where Jean flees to).

Shortly afterwards, the Germans occupied much of France, as they had in the First World War. There was little resistance, for it seemed inevitable that, this time, the German army would win. Soon, Germany would rule the whole of Europe.

1 ✳ Paris, February 1943

When the Germans took over, in June 1940, I was twelve. Every day, the Germans staged a big march, with a military band, along our biggest street, the Champs Elysées.

"We're part of Germany now," Mum told me.

"Does that mean they'll send Dad home?" I asked.

"I don't know."

Her voice was so sad, I didn't ask again. My dad had been a prisoner of war for six months. We didn't know where he was. We didn't even know if he was alive.

Within a week, half my friends were gone. Many people went to the South, which the Germans didn't occupy at first. Mum and I talked about going ourselves. We had relatives there. Now and then my uncle sent us food parcels. But the South was a long way to go. And what would happen if Dad came home? How would he find us?

Mum and I live in a small flat, just the two of

us. We have electricity and running water – some of the time. The first winter of the occupation was so cold, we spent half our time in bed, huddled together for warmth. The next two were worse. We're hungry all the time. I'm fourteen, but I don't weigh any more than I did at twelve. Mum's all skin and bones. If Dad did come back, he wouldn't recognise her.

Mum has a job in a laundry, but it doesn't pay enough for many extras. Even potatoes are hard to come by. Often, we eat rutabagas – swedes. Before the war, they were only given to cows. But I shouldn't complain. Some people have it far worse than us. The Germans hate Jews, don't ask me why. They've renamed all the streets which used to be named after Jews. Books by Jewish authors have all been burnt.

A girl called Sophie used to live across the street. We were in the same class. One day, she showed up at school with a yellow star on her tunic. All Jews over the age of six had to wear them.

Early last year, Sophie's father was taken to a camp in Drancy, on the edge of Paris. She was worried sick about him. I was friends with Sophie, but last summer, in the holidays, I didn't see much of her. I had other things on my mind.

You see, last June, Monsieur Laval, the deputy Prime Minister, announced a new measure, the Relève. It sounded like a wonderful thing. For every three Frenchmen who volunteered to go and work in Germany, the Germans would release one prisoner of war! My dad might come home!

"Don't get too excited, Jean," my mother warned. "Not many men want to go and work like slaves in German factories."

In August, the first prisoners came back. My father wasn't one of them. Even so, my hopes stayed high. But that was it. No more prisoners appeared. The BBC, broadcasting from London, urged people not to volunteer for the Relève. All over town, posters for the Relève were torn down or covered in graffiti.

We used to think the British would surrender soon. But now the Americans are in the war. The Russians are against Germany too. People are starting to say the Germans are losing. The food shortages and power cuts are getting worse.

With those things going on, I didn't notice that I hadn't seen Sophie for a while. Then, when school started back up, Sophie wasn't there. People said that she, her mother, and her younger brother had been taken to the camp in Drancy. From there, people say, they were taken to another camp, in Germany.

"Jean," Mum told me yesterday, "things are going to get worse. I've been writing to your uncle Henri, in the South. He says there's enough food to go round. I think you should go there. It's a long journey, but a friend of his can take you."

I haven't seen my uncle or my cousins for years.

"I don't want to go," I told Mum. "I won't go unless you come with me."

"I have to stay here for when your father comes back. But it's not safe for you. Look what happened to Sophie."

"But she's Jewish!"

"And you're a strong boy. If you don't get ill or starve to death, the Germans might make you work for them. Look at the soldiers in the streets. They get younger every month. At least if you were in the South, and the Germans tried to take you, your uncle would be able to hide you."

"I won't go without you!" I swore.

But today I saw a headline on a newspaper.

The Relève, it said, was over. I stopped and looked closer. There was a new law, the STO (Service du Travail Obligatoire), which ordered young Frenchmen to go and work in Germany.

Prisoners of war have to work, too, even though that's against the international rules of war. No more prisoners are coming home.

"Dad's not coming back," I tell Mum when I get home. "I'll go to the South, but only if you come with me."

Mum refuses. "I'd just be another mouth to feed. You can help your uncle with his farm. I'm not strong enough. Better if I stay here and work in the laundry, wait for your father."

I don't want to abandon her, but Mum insists.

"Be strong," she says. "Don't do anything foolish. One day, all of this will just be a bad memory."

"I don't want to be a coward," I say.

"Sometimes," Mum warns, "it's brave to be a coward and cowardly to be brave."

I don't understand what she means.

2 ✳ Bandits

My uncle's friend is called Paul Lurcat. He's a quiet man with steely black hair and oily skin.

His left leg was crushed by a tractor when he was my age. He calls it his 'lucky limp'. Lucky because it stopped him going to war. If he'd gone, he might be a prisoner like my dad.

Paul transports cattle to Paris in a small lorry. It's a two-day journey. We've only been stopped once. German soldiers wanted to know what we had in the back. Paul told them. Nothing but a little hay. They took a look to make sure that he was telling the truth.

The empty lorry passes field after field. Rain pours down. It's a cold, late winter afternoon. We keep passing patches of woodland. Paul always speeds up when this happens. I don't know why.

I begin to recognise the area. We're near where my uncle and cousins live. We're driving through an area of dense woods when Paul swears.

"What is it?" I ask.

"Probably nothing, Jean. Don't worry." He puts his foot on the accelerator, then thinks better of it. All of a sudden I can see what he's seen. A group of shabby figures are coming out of the woods. They wear dark greatcoats or ancient oilskins. The tallest one holds a rifle. Not a shiny new one, like Germans carry. This is huge, ancient, a relic of the last war. He points it straight at us. Paul brakes.

"Stay there," he tells me. "I'll sort this out."

"But who are they?" I ask.

"Bandits," he tells me.

The tall man waves his rifle around. He signals Paul to get out of the lorry. Paul obeys, but can't move quickly. Through the open door, I strain to hear what the men are saying.

"What have you got in the back, eh?"

"What business is it of yours?" Paul ask.

"Watch your mouth, dead leg. We're the official Maquis."

"There's no such thing," Paul tells them. "How about letting me get on my way?"

I don't hear the reply. Suddenly a youth jumps into the cabin next to me. He has long hair, bad teeth and a fiendish grin.

"Why aren't you in school?" he asks, pulling something out of his pocket. The lad's sixteen or seventeen. In his hand he has a big, rusty revolver.

"What's in the back?" he asks, putting the revolver against my head. I can feel its cold barrel on my temple. I'm terrified.

"Nothing," I reply. "The Germans have searched us already. We're on our way to collect cattle."

Outside, I can hear Paul saying, "There's only hay in there. I transport cattle from the Southern zone to Paris. That's all I do."

"We'll see about that," the men's leader says.

I'm used to German soldiers with guns. But the Germans are disciplined. These men speak my language but they look wild. Rain pours down. The lorry rattles as the men get in the back. They start searching.

Suddenly, I hear whoops of delight. They've found something. What can it be? The bandits are bound to shoot us both, to keep us quiet. My legs start to shake.

When the men come back, they're carrying paper packages. The packages must have been hidden beneath the hay. I don't know what's inside them. The youth with the bad teeth grins again. He gestures for Paul to get back into the cabin.

Scowling, Paul obeys. The youth reaches into

an inside pocket for his revolver. I think about getting out, making a run for it. But there are six of them, and they have at least one rifle.

"Here." He holds something out. "Take this." He wasn't going for a revolver. It was a piece of paper. Paul drives off. I look in the rear view mirror, amazed at our luck. The bandits have disappeared into the woods and we're still alive.

3 ✳ The Maquis

"What is it?" I ask Paul, pointing at the piece of paper, which has fallen to the floor.

"A receipt," he says. "According to this, after the war I'll be reimbursed for my losses. It's rubbish." He tears it up.

"What did they take?" I want to know.

"Tobacco." Now I understand why the men were so happy. Tobacco is as precious as gold–dust, even though you can't eat it.

"Why did you have tobacco?" I ask.

"For profit!" Paul snaps. "Don't you know anything? You're only meant to sell cattle to the Germans, who pay low prices. On the black market, people will give anything for good meat, and tobacco's more use than money."

"But I thought you transported cattle for the Germans?"

"I do. What the Germans don't know is that I do a little trading for myself. Every trip, a farmer gives me an extra cow or two. I give him tobacco, which he can trade or smoke. Good tobacco, not the dried up sticks and herbs that you get in the ration. I take the cow and trade it for more tobacco. In the end, everybody's happy, even the Germans."

"But what if you get caught?" I ask.

"Why would I get caught?" Paul says. It all sounds risky to me, but I shut up about it.

"Were those men the Resistance?" I ask Paul after a while.

He shakes his head. "The Resistance is a myth. Did you ever come across the Resistance in Paris?"

"No, but I thought that was because there were so many Germans there."

"There were no Germans here until recently. Still, we never saw any resistance. The Free French are with De Gaulle in London or fighting for the Allies. People say there's some resistance in the north, but nobody knows for sure."

"Then who were those bandits?" I ask.

"They were réfractaires, deserters."

"Then why do they call themselves the Maquis?"

"I don't know," says Paul, in a sneering voice. "Nobody had heard of the Maquis a month ago. Then Laval brought in the STO law. Men were ordered to go to Germany. So now some of them hide out in the woods when they hear the Germans are coming. They go back to work when the Germans have gone."

"Then they're farmworkers, like my uncle?"

"A few of them, maybe."

We pass through Villefranche. It's a small village which has a school, two streets, three shops and a marketplace with a Mairie (mayor's office). A mile beyond it, Paul's lorry turns up the rough track to my uncle's farm.

It stops raining. The sun pokes out from behind a cloud. A beautiful young woman with curly brown hair comes running up to the lorry.

It takes me a moment to recognise my cousin. When I last saw Nina, she was the age I am now. Now she's a woman of almost twenty-one.

"I brought him, like I promised," Paul tells her.

"You're a wonder!" Nina kisses Paul on the cheek then hugs me. "Jean, how thin you are! We'll have to feed you up!" My cousin Philippe and Uncle Henri are out in the fields, she tells me. I offer to go and help them.

"Nonsense. You must be tired from your journey. Let's take your things to your bedroom." Nina leads me upstairs. Paul follows.

The room is small. I will have to share it with my cousin, Philippe. He gets back as I'm having a wash. Philippe has grown too. He's stocky, but shorter than Nina. His dark hair is thick. He's unshaven – you wouldn't call it a beard – and has spots. He's nineteen, but looks younger.

"You'd better not snore!" Philippe warns. I promise not to.

* * * * *

For dinner we have rabbit stew. There's no swede in it. Instead, there are carrots and onions and potatoes and lots of meat.

"It's the best meal I've had since the war began!" I tell Nina. As I pick out the rabbit bones, I explain to Nina, Philippe, Paul and Uncle Henri about life in Paris. I tell them how we wear wooden clogs because there's no leather for shoes.

"Paris is the Germans' holiday city, the place they all want to come to on leave. They get fine wine and caviar. Mum and I celebrate if we get half a dozen eggs. We have ration books for food, but never get enough to eat. There's hardly ever any meat or cheese, unless you use the black market." Everyone looks at Paul when I mention the black market. I go on. "Some people keep rabbits in their flats, for eating. And chickens. I've even heard of people eating guinea pigs."

"Guinea pigs!" Nina exclaims. "Do they keep frogs in the bath, too?"

"What's it like, having the Germans there all the time?" Philippe wants to know.

"You get used to them," I say. Philippe gives me a look as if to say 'I wouldn't'. So I try to explain.

"At first, the only change was the clocks going forward an hour, so we were on Third Reich time. A few places shut down, like museums, or the post office. But they reopened in a day or two. We were off school for nearly a month and that was great.

"The Germans kept trying to be nice to us, like they're our guests. But we'd have fun, giving them directions to the wrong place or scribbling jokes and swear-words on their posters.

"There's no petrol, so now there are bikes everywhere. Pretty ladies wear trousers so they can ride them. My bike got..."

"I don't want to hear about bikes!" Philippe interrupts.

"I do," Nina says. "Tell me."

"Two weeks into the occupation, this gang of lads stole my bike. There's no petrol for private cars, so bikes are the best way to get around. People kept stealing them to sell on the black market. That's stopped now, because there are loads of new bikes around. People say there are two million in the city. They're everywhere. Only trouble is, a bike costs more than a car used to. I can't afford one."

"You can borrow mine while you're here," Nina offers. "But, be warned, it's a boneshaker."

I thank her.

"What about the Resistance?" Philippe asks. "There must be some resistance!"

"There was one demonstration," I tell him. "The Germans arrested a few people. Some people talk big. They say they're only waiting for the right moment to fight back, but they don't do much. I know it sounds strange, but Paris is like it used to be, only quieter. The Métro shuts down at eleven. If you miss it, you have to stay where you are because of the curfew."

"At least we don't have a curfew here," Paul says.

"There's nowhere to go at night anyway,"

Nina complains.

Soon, the meal is over. Uncle Henri goes to sleep in his chair. Paul helps Nina to wash up.

"Is Nina Paul's girlfriend?" I ask Philippe later, when we've gone to bed.

"He'd like her to be," Philippe tells me. "What happened on the way here? Paul wouldn't tell the story properly."

I tell Philippe about the Maquis. "The only one I got a really good look at was this lad with bad teeth and long hair." I describe his grin.

"That's Georges Guitry," Philippe tells me. "I was at school with him. He's a real vagabond."

"He's the same age as you?"

"Two years younger."

"Then he can't be hiding from the STO."

"No, Georges will be doing it for the fun of it, because it's better than working on a farm. I wondered where he'd got to."

I leave it a moment, then ask a question.

"What do you know about the Maquis?"

But Philippe has gone to sleep. At first, I think he's pretending. However, within minutes, he's snoring loudly.

4 ✳ June, 1943

It's taken a while to get used to living in Villefranche. At school there was nobody my age. Hardly anybody went to school, so I've stopped going, too. At first I was so weak and thin that Uncle Henri wouldn't let me help on the farm. But I'm eating good food for the first time in years and I've put on weight. I still look young for my age, but I help as much as I can, digging, carrying, feeding animals. The work's hard but I prefer it to studying.

Hard work stops me thinking about how much I miss my mum. She wrote me a long letter on my fifteenth birthday, last week. She wrote that my being here was for the best. Maybe it is. I try not to think about her too much. I try not to think about Dad. I still end up thinking about both of them all of the time.

Most able-bodied men are away. The STO makes exceptions for essential workers, but the rules keep changing. My uncle lost two men just before I arrived. One went to Germany, the other vanished.

Two miles from my uncle's farm, the Germans have taken over a chateau. We can see the big house, high on a hill. And they can see us. Because of this, Uncle Henri can't employ workers who shouldn't be here. Even Nina helps out, though she has more than enough work to do elsewhere.

I get on better with Nina than my other cousin. Philippe doesn't want a sidekick four years younger than him. Nina's six years older than me, but she's always glad of company. Their mum died of influenza, two years ago. Since then, Nina's done the housework. She also takes on any jobs she can get. Nina mends clothes in exchange for make-up, or material. She helps in the village store when the owner's away trying to find new stock. That's how Nina met the German captain from the chateau.

One evening, Nina tells the rest of us how the captain came into the shop that day.

"He's so young to be a captain. I know you told us that German soldiers were getting younger, Jean, but he can't be more than – oh – twenty-four. And he speaks good French."

"He'd better not speak to me!" Philippe insists. "And you shouldn't speak to him either!"

"What am I supposed to do?" Nina replies, offended. "Ignore him? He bought lots of things."

"I'm surprised he was able to find anything worth buying," my uncle says. "I never can."

"He's trying to buy our friendship," Philippe comments. "But he's our enemy, no matter how nice he seems."

"I agree," Nina tells him. "But there are bound to be good Germans as well as bad Germans, aren't there?"

"The only good German is a dead German," Philippe says, and my uncle nods his head. The subject is closed.

* * * * *

Next day, I'm picking peas near the road when an open-topped jeep pulls up beside me. I know at once who it is. The man in the captain's uniform is young and handsome.

"Why aren't you in school?" he asks.

"We have to get the pea harvest in," I tell him.

"Your schooling's important."

"Not as important as feeding the troops," I reply, sarcastically.

The captain smiles. "You've got me there. I'd better let that pass. They tell me that the girl who sometimes works at the store lives on this farm. Are you her brother?"

"Cousin," I tell him, then wish I'd lied. In Paris, I always lied if a German asked me a question. It was a point of honour.

"Where is she now?" the captain wants to know.

"I don't know." This is a lie. Nina's doing the same as me, two fields away. The captain only has to look around to find her.

"When you see your cousin, say I have some work for her. She's to come to the chateau, any time before dark."

"I'll tell her," I say.

As soon as the jeep is out of sight, I run over to the field where Nina is working. I let her know what's just happened.

"Did Dad or Philippe see him?" Nina asks, worried.

"No. They're still on the other side of the farm."

"Then don't tell them."

"You're not going to go?" I ask her.

"What choice do I have?" Nina asks. "The Germans are in charge. The captain can make me do what he likes. The government's forcing women to go into all kinds of jobs that men have left. I don't want to work in a factory in

Toulouse."

"It'd be better than working for the Germans," I say.

"We're all working for the Germans," Nina says, sadly. "Half the food we're harvesting goes to Germany. More, if we don't hide it carefully. Jean, you start supper tonight. I'll cycle to the chateau, see what the captain wants. He looks like a soft touch to me. You never know, we might do well out of this."

Uncle Henri doesn't finish work until late that evening. When he comes in, Philippe's not with him.

"Where's Nina?" my uncle asks, seeing me cooking. (Nina's taught me to make simple soups and stews.)

"She had a job to do. Where's Philippe?"

"Gone to see somebody. He'll eat when he comes in."

Nina doesn't return until after I'm in bed. Neither does Philippe. Later, he wakes me up. He smells of smoke.

"What's that smell?" I ask.

"Fireworks," Philippe says. "You'll understand tomorrow." He sings softly to himself, a patriotic song.

I fall into uneasy sleep.

5 ✳ Explosions

Next morning there's news. Pierre, my uncle's oldest worker, has seen it for himself. Just beyond Villefranche, part of the railway line was blown up. Sabotage. Carriages bearing German tanks were nearly derailed.

"Pity they missed them," Uncle Henri says.

"No it isn't," Philippe says, sounding knowledgeable. "If the Maquis had destroyed the tanks, the Germans would have rounded up everybody in the village and started shooting people, like they did in Bordeaux. Do you want that?"

"I suppose not," Uncle Henri says, in a suspicious voice.

"Are you sure it was the Maquis?" Nina asks.

"Who else would it be?" Philippe snaps back. I recognise the proud edge in his voice, but Nina doesn't seem to.

"The Germans want me to work for them," she blurts out.

"They what?" Uncle Henri asks, angrily.

"Cooking, helping to deal with suppliers, things like that."

"I hope you refused!" Philippe demands.

"I don't have a choice. They say if I don't work for them there, I'll be assigned somewhere else soon. And they're going to pay me well. I might be able to get some extras – jam, coffee, that kind of thing."

"I'd rather starve!" Philippe insists.

"You don't know what starvation is!" Nina turns to me. "What about you, Jean? You know what it's like to be hungry. Would you rather starve?"

"I'm staying out of this," I tell her.

"You're wise," my uncle says. "There's one thing I don't understand, Nina. How did they come to choose you?"

"The captain saw me working in the village shop."

"How many hours a day will it be?"

"Only eight. Jean will do more of the housework when I'm gone. Won't you, Jean?"

Before I can reply, Philippe answers for me. "Jean's nearly a man. You shouldn't be training him to do woman's work!"

We finish breakfast in silence.

Two days later, Nina comes home from the

chateau with some terrible news.

"I overheard them talking," she tells us. "The Germans have captured a big Resistance leader and tortured him to death."

"Who?" I ask. "Do you remember the name?"

"It's the same as yours. Jean... Moulin, I think."

I groan. Everyone in Paris knew who Jean Moulin was – the man who De Gaulle sent to coordinate the Conseil National de la Résistance. If the Germans have caught and killed him, then the Resistance is in a bad way.

"They talked about this in front of you?" Philippe asks.

"In German. They don't know that I learnt it at school."

"Make sure that you don't let on," her brother orders.

"What do you think I am, stupid?"

Philippe shrugs. To watch these two is to watch a squabble which has been going on since Philippe was born. My uncle pours each of us a glass of wine. We toast the memory of Jean Moulin. After a few glasses, Philippe's tongue becomes loose.

"The Resistance is weak. Our only hope is the Maquis."

"What about the Allies?" Nina asks.

"It'll be years before they get here. We have to get rid of the Germans ourselves."

"With what?" Uncle Henri teases. "Big sticks and a few guns left over from the first war? The Maquis aren't the Resistance. They're deserters from the STO, hiding out in the woods. They're a joke!"

Philippe gives my uncle a hard look. "I'll be twenty soon. The Germans will try to draft me. Which would you prefer me to do – go to Germany, or join the Maquis in the woods?"

Before my uncle can answer, Nina speaks. "You might not have to go to Germany. I talked to the captain. He says..."

"It's bad enough that you work for Germans!" Philippe interrupts. "You don't have to talk with them!"

He stomps off to his bed. I wait until I think he's asleep before I go up. But Philippe's awake, brooding.

"You know I've been out with them, don't you?" he says.

"The Maquis?" I reply, timidly. "I guessed, yes."

He tells me all about the railway raid the other night.

"I planted one of the bombs." He describes the explosions in vivid detail. "There are boys your age joining in, Jean. Younger."

"Is that right?"

"Soon, the moment will come. You'll have to decide what to do."

"How do you mean?" I ask.

"You're either for us, or against us. Remember that."

I don't reply. Is it so simple? Most people agree with Paul Lurcat and Uncle Henri. The Maquis are just bandits, using the war as an excuse to steal. The real Resistance is in the North. Nobody knows how strong it is.

Sabotage sounds like a good idea, except that the Germans often shoot innocent people when they can't catch the saboteurs. And I don't want to become a thief.

Yet maybe Philippe's right. It's better to be a bandit than a lackey of the Germans. But where does that leave Nina? And where does it leave me?

6 ✸ August, 1943

It happens as I'm helping to herd two cows onto Paul's lorry. Suddenly, there's a shotgun in my face.

"Get on the floor and stay there!" a masked man tells me.

Paul hobbles out of the lorry to find out what's going on. "Not again!" he says.

Paul isn't armed. The masked man hits Paul on the head with the butt of his rifle. Then he shuts the back of the lorry. Another masked man gets into the driver's seat. Across the field, my Uncle Henri sees what's happening. He runs over. But it's too late. The two men have driven off in Paul's lorry, with my uncle's cattle. We help Paul up and go back to the farm.

"They were a different lot from before," Paul says.

"They're all bandits," my uncle replies. "What's the difference?"

Paul has noticed something. "Where's Nina?" he asks.

Uncle Henri explains about her working in the chateau. Nina isn't interested in being Paul's girlfriend. She'd told me this during one of our talks. But she hasn't told Paul.

"How could she work in such a place?" he asks.

"She has no choice," Uncle Henri tells him.

I don't know if that's true or not. For Nina is very cheerful when she comes back from the chateau every night. And she keeps bringing goodies home – jam, coffee, even chocolate.

"Aren't you taking a risk, stealing these?" Uncle Henri asks that night. "You know what the Germans do to thieves."

"No risk. I promise, Daddy."

When we're alone, Nina tells me what I've already guessed.

"The stuff I bring home, they're gifts from Helmut."

"Helmut?"

"The captain. I spend a lot of time talking to him. He's not really a soldier, you know. He was at university, studying Art History. He stayed out of the war for a while. Then he had to join the Army. But he's from a rich family, so they made him a captain and kept him away from the fighting."

"Lucky Helmut," I say.

"You'd like him if you got to know him. It's not his fault that he's at war with us."

"I guess not."

She starts to say something else but then thinks better of it.

"Don't tell Philippe that I've been talking to Helmut."

"I won't."

"I may have to put in extra hours at the chateau. It'll mean more work for you. I'm sorry."

"It's OK," I reply. I should be grateful. I'm well fed, fit and healthy. I'm much better off than I would be in Paris. But I feel uncomfortable.

There's a knock on the door. It's Paul, for Nina. I decide that this is a good time to go to bed. But when I go up, Philippe is already in the bedroom. And he's not alone.

A shabby figure with long hair and bad teeth sits on my bed.

"This is Georges," Philippe says. I nod a hello.

"We've met already." Georges Guitry doesn't recognise me, so I tell him, "Last time I saw you, you were holding a gun against my head."

Georges remembers. "Oh yes, the tobacco

raid, back in February. Sorry about that, but it was for a good cause."

"You're taking a chance being here," I tell him. "Paul is downstairs. Remember Paul, who you robbed this morning?"

"You mean your uncle's cattle? That wasn't us," Georges protests. "It was a faux Maquis. They're thieves, pretending to be us. It's happening a lot."

"According to Paul," I tell Georges, "you're the fakes."

"Paul's a smuggler, a black marketeer. He deserves what he gets."

"The war makes smugglers out of many people," Philippe reminds Georges. "Jean, leave us alone, would you? We have business to discuss."

"But..."

"You're too young to be involved. Go on, leave!" I go back downstairs. Luckily, Paul's gone. Nina has told him how she feels.

"I said that he wasn't right for me. He asked if it was his leg. I said no. He asked if there was someone else. I said there wasn't. Of course, there is."

"Really?" I mutter, not wanting to be told any more secrets. But it's too late.

"Oh Jean, can't you guess? It's Helmut, the captain. We spend every minute that we can together. It's wonderful. When the war's over, we're going to marry! Aren't you happy for me?"

"Yes, I guess," I say, though I'm far from happy.

"We're not doing anything wrong."

"Maybe not," I say. "But you've only known him a few weeks. And it's dangerous. In Paris, girls who went out with Germans got called horrible names. People said that terrible things would happen to them after the war."

"We're in love, Jean. It has nothing to do with the war."

"If I were you, I wouldn't tell anyone else."

"I won't, but I trust you. It'll be our secret."

I hear the back door closing. Georges has left. Back in the bedroom, Philippe has gone, too. I get between the sheets, but sleep won't come. Too many secrets, keeping me awake.

7 ✳ The Milice

The Germans have occupied the Southern Zone for nine months now. Officially, the French are still in charge, but the Germans run everything, like they did in Paris. They've even set up a French version of the Nazi SS, called the Milice. The Milice are meant to go after the réfractaires, the men on the run from the STO. They're also after the Maquis, except that the Maquis aren't meant to exist.

Nobody likes the Milice. They're French, and they're volunteers. They make us think badly of ourselves. The Germans have demanded another half million men from France to work in Germany. Hundreds of Milice and police search the woods and mountains. Thousands of réfractaires are captured.

I first see the Milice in the Market square one hot day in August. Their uniform is very French. They wear khaki shirts, black ties, trousers and jackets in dark blue and, of course, a black beret. Their emblem is a white Y, the mark of the goat. There are six of them and they're in a hurry.

"What are they doing?" I ask Philippe.

"There's a rumour that the Maquis are hiding in the woods a mile away."

"How do you know that?" I ask him.

Philippe smiles. "I started the rumour."

The six men set off in an open-topped lorry. As they leave I glance at the leather holsters on their belts. Something is in each one, but it doesn't look like a gun. I ask Philippe what it is.

"Paper!" he tells me, then explains. "The Germans don't have enough guns to give out at the moment. I think they have one rifle between them!"

"Will the Maquis be able to beat them?"

"They won't find the Maquis," Philippe tells me. Then he signals to somebody standing beside the Mairie. "Clear!"

A truck drives into the market place. I recognise the tall man driving and the youth in the passenger seat. Georges Guitry. He's holding his revolver. People stare.

The Mairie has double doors. One is open. The tall Maquisard kicks open the other. Then the five of them pile in.

"What's in there?" I ask Philippe. I can't believe there's anything worth stealing.

"Our dignity," Philippe replies.

Five minutes later, the Maquis band return from the Mairie. They begin to hand out bits of paper. Georges thrusts one into my hand. It's a recruiting leaflet.

Men who come to the Maquis to fight live badly, with food hard to find. They are cut off from their families and must not write to them.

Bring two shirts, two pairs of underpants, two pairs of woollen socks, a light sweater, a scarf, a heavy sweater, a woollen blanket, an extra pair of shoes, shoelaces, needles, thread, buttons, safety pins, soap, a canteen, a knife and fork, a torch, a compass, a weapon if possible, and also a sleeping bag if possible. Wear a warm suit, a beret, a raincoat and a good pair of hobnailed boots.

"It doesn't sound like much of a life," I tell Philippe as the Maquisards get back into their truck. They drive off in the opposite direction to that of the Milice.

"It'll be my life soon," he says.

Next month, Philippe turns twenty. Any day now, he'll get his STO papers.

The Maquis have trashed the Mayor's office. They've taken nothing but a couple of weapons. The Mayor and his men have offered no resistance. Nor were they surprised. All over the Southern Zone there are stories of similar raids. There aren't enough Milice to keep the Maquis in line. Fewer people call the Maquis "bandits" these days. They might think it, but they keep their mouths shut.

Philippe goes off. I hang about the market. As a favour, Nina's working in the store today. I want to walk her home.

That's how I happen to see the Milice return.

They've got a prisoner. He's a réfractaire, not much older than Philippe. As they march him to the cells, I see how badly they've beaten him up.

At least the Maquis didn't hurt anybody. Philippe's right. You have to choose which side you're on, and there's only one side worth choosing.

The Germans arrive to inspect the damage at the Mairie. As Nina locks up, I see the captain in the town square, looking at us. Nina turns and sees her boyfriend, but ignores him. She's playing it safe. I'm the only one who knows she's engaged.

But the captain isn't as clever as Nina. We're halfway home when his jeep pulls up alongside us.

"You two must be hot. Can I offer you a ride?"

Before I can say "no", Nina accepts. If I let her go alone, it will make their relationship obvious. So I get in.

Helmut is in a cheerful mood. "The Milice – what a lot of country bumpkins they are! Those idiots couldn't find a Maquis if they burnt down a whole forest to smoke them out. All that lot are interested in is having a little power. They're welcome to it."

"You should turn here," I say, pointing to the farm. Helmut ignores me. I see where we're heading now the chateau.

"I'll be glad when the war is over," Helmut says. "Won't you?"

"As long as you send my dad home," I tell him. Helmut smiles sympathetically. "Nina's told me about him. I wish I could get him back, but he's so far away. Still, maybe I can help you. Nina says she's told you about us."

"Yes."

"I wondered whether you'd like some work at the chateau, too. I'm very understaffed. We could use you. And it pays well."

"No, thank you," I tell him.

"It's your choice," he says, as we pull up in the cobble-stoned courtyard. The chateau's bigger than it looks from the bottom of the hill. The captain smiles and ushers me inside.

"Would you mind giving Nina and me a few minutes together before you go back? I'll get the cook to fix you something to eat." Nina smiles apologetically. It's more than a few minutes, of course. The cook brings me wine, cooked meat, fresh bread and cheese. I don't like the look on her face as she serves me. The food's good, yet I can't enjoy it properly. When Nina finally returns, she says that Helmut will drive us back to the farm.

"No!" I say firmly. "We've already risked being seen."

"I'll think up a story," Nina says.

"No. We'll walk."

We walk.

"It didn't look like there were many German soldiers in the garrison," I say to Nina once we're out of sight of the chateau.

"There aren't. And the few Helmut has are in their teens."

I say nothing, wondering what to do with

this information.

"Don't you like Helmut?" Nina asks.

"He'd be all right if he wasn't German."

"You sound like Philippe," she says.

There are a lot of things I could say, but I stay quiet.

The following morning, Philippe gets his papers from the STO. He's to go to Germany on September the 20th, the day after his twentieth birthday.

8 ✳ Autumn, 1943

"There's no point in me hanging around," Philippe says, a week before his birthday. "I might as well go now."

"I can talk to the captain," Nina offers again. "Maybe he can pull a few strings..."

"No!" Philippe protests.

"The truth is," Nina says, "you really want to join the Maquis, to go and live in the woods like a tramp."

"Maybe I do," Philippe says.

"And what about the winter, when you'll freeze?"

"I'll manage."

"And our father, how will he manage?"

"At least he's got Jean. The war will be over by next year's harvest. You'll see. The Germans can't last much longer."

"That's not what..." Nina stops herself saying Helmut's name, "...they're saying at the chateau."

They stop talking as Uncle Henri comes in.

He gets the radio out of its hiding place in the cupboard, turns on the BBC.

If you own a radio, you're meant to declare it to the authorities, but my uncle hasn't. The Germans jam foreign broadcasts but we still get them, only faintly. Every night, at nine, the BBC broadcast the news in French. If we were caught listening to a foreign station, the Germans would seize the radio. Uncle Henri would be fined or arrested. But, like everyone else, we ignore the law and tune in.

The Italian government has agreed an armistice with the Allies.

Philippe laughs. "Do you hear? The Italians have surrendered. Now the Germans are on their own."

"The Allies still have to fight the Japanese," Uncle Henri reminds him.

"Not round here they don't. I'm telling you, they'll invade France in no time."

That night, going to bed, I see that Philippe has packed a bag. The next morning, he's gone.

* * * * *

Weeks pass. According to the BBC, the war is still going badly for Germany. Around here, more and more men are joining the Maquis, even though it's getting colder. Hardly anybody has anything bad to say about the Maquis any more. Everybody knows somebody who's hiding in the woods.

Now and then, Philippe sneaks home. He has a bath, a meal, washes some clothes. He boasts to me about things he's done. The Villefranche Maquis has stolen a jeep and a lorry. To cap that, they've taken three barrels of petrol. They're planning another railway sabotage, he says, or maybe a big grain theft.

On French radio, Monsieur Laval, the deputy prime minister, announces an amnesty. Any réfractaire who gives himself up will not have to go to Germany. People whose sons have already gone to Germany (nearly three-quarters of a million of them) are furious. It isn't fair, they say. But war isn't fair. Anybody can work that one out.

* * * * *

The news says that a quarter of a million prisoners of war are working for the Germans. Maybe my dad's one of them. Uncle Henri urges Philippe to give himself up. Philippe won't.

Yet, as it gets colder, Philippe comes home more and more. It's the same story with many other Maquisards. There are no leaves on the trees, making it harder for them to hide. More of them would be caught, except that nobody helps the Milice as they search. The South's like Paris in the early days of the occupation.

Everybody gives the Milice the wrong directions or delays them with stupid questions. The Maquis hide in areas not covered by maps. It's easy for the Milice to get lost, even if they're in the right area. Often they're not.

Nina is nervous. She doesn't want Helmut to find out that she's sheltering a réfractaire. Philippe, when he's home, makes things worse by asking lots of questions about the chateau.

"How many men are there? Where do they keep their arms? Do they have much food? What times is it empty?"

Nina either avoids answering or keeps her replies vague. She's terrified the Maquis will raid the chateau while she's there.

"If you're a real Maquisard, you should be in the woods," she tells her brother.

"What do you want me to do?" Philippe replies. "Freeze to death?"

Yet a few days later, he's gone again. It's November. When Philippe has been gone nearly a week, we hear great news on the BBC. At Oyonnax, not many miles away, the Maquis have taken over the town. They blocked off access roads and captured the post office, fire station, gendarmerie – even the German commissariat. Then they held a parade through the town to mark Armistice day, the anniversary of the ending of the last war. A day later, heads held high, they left the town. A triumph.

Two days after that, Philippe returns. He's full of what happened in Oyonnax. At the dinner table he tells me about it.

"There were Maquisards from all over the South. Nearly three hundred of us. We all had uniforms."

"Where did you get them?" I ask.

"The last war. Or they were stolen, or home made. Who cares? We left behind a wreath with a message on it. *From tomorrow's victors to those of 14-18.*"

"What did the Germans do?" I ask.

"The Germans weren't there that day."

Suddenly, I'm less impressed. "Did you fight the Milice, or the Gendarmes?" I ask.

"There were no Milice. The Gendarmes

weren't going to get in our way. Did you hear De Gaulle on the radio?"

I'd heard. For the first time, De Gaulle praised the Maquis. At last, Philippe feels like a hero, though all he's done is to march into a town with no opposition.

* * * * *

After that, he's gone for weeks. All day I work outside, in the cold and biting wind, looking after animals, fixing fences, watching out for thieves. The war will soon be over and I've done nothing to help defeat the Germans. Maybe I should join Philippe in the woods, even though my uncle needs me. I hear stories of sabotage and heroic raids. Some must be true.

Yet, all the time, men are returning from the woods and going back to their homes, where they keep their heads down. People in the village turn a blind eye. It's cold, and not even the Milice have the energy to track down réfractaires.

It must be cold in Germany too. I wonder whether my father has warm clothes.

9 ✳ 1944

One Sunday in January, when I go downstairs for breakfast, Nina isn't there.

"She left a note," Uncle Henri complains.

"*Needed at the chateau.* She shouldn't be working for them on a Sunday! I've a good mind to go up there and get her!"

"Don't go," I tell him. "I'm sure she'll be home soon."

But Nina isn't back in time to cook lunch. Uncle Henri's angry. He's killed a chicken specially. But he hates to cook and I've never done roast chicken before.

"I'm going up there!" he says.

Uncle Henri has no idea that Nina is engaged to Helmut. If he were to go up to the chateau, he might see something, work it out. I can't let that happen.

"I'll go," I offer.

Uncle Henri thinks about it for a moment. "I suppose that'll be all right," he says. "Tell her to hurry back. I don't want this chicken to go to waste."

"I'll tell her."

Nina hasn't taken her bicycle, so I use it to cycle up to the chateau. What Uncle Henri and the Maquis don't know is how few Germans there are there. The security is a joke. And Nina doesn't have a lot to do. She's here because of Helmut, not work. As I cycle into the courtyard, the first thing I hear is her laughter.

Where are the weapons? I wonder, as I look around. Where's the guard? When I came before, there was one at the main door, but there isn't today. I try the handle on the main door. It's locked. I could knock, but, instead, I walk around the chateau, away from the sound of Nina's voice.

I've not explored this place before. When I visited my uncle's farm as a child, the chateau belonged to a rich family. They fled over the border to Switzerland as soon as the war started. Then the place was empty for a while. Parts still seem shut off. Round the back, there are two outhouses. I open the door to one. It's full of coal. Tons and tons of coal. The Maquis could burn it instead of freezing to death on the mountains.

One of the downstairs rooms in the chateau

has iron bars over the windows. Is it some kind of prison? I spot wires going from the window, up to the roof. It must be their radio room. Finally, I find what I'm looking for. A back door. The servants' entrance. It might be easy to sneak up here, at night. I try the handle. It's open.

"Halt!" says a German voice. "Who goes there?" I nearly wet myself, but then I remember that I have a good reason to be here.

"I'm Nina's cousin, Jean. My uncle is worried about her. She's not meant to be working today, but I think she's here."

In the hall, a German soldier steps out of the shadows and smiles. He's young, younger than Philippe.

"You do, do you?" he says, looking amused. "Why's that?"

"I could hear her laughing."

"Wait there," the soldier says. "I'll see if I can find her." He goes off, leaving the door unguarded. His footsteps echo through the dark, dusty chateau. Quickly, I walk down the corridor to my left, counting the number of doors. At the fourth one, I can hear the tap-tap-tap of Morse code. The radio room. I try the door. It's unlocked. But I don't go in. That would be pushing my luck too far.

I get back to the hall just as Nina arrives. She looks embarrassed. I explain why I've come.

"Is that the time?" Nina says. "I'm sorry, I thought I'd be back earlier. The cook's ill. That's why I came to help." I don't know whether to believe her or not. "I've made stew. There's big portions for you and Dad. Why don't you take it down on the bike? I'll follow in a while."

"I told Uncle Henri I'd bring you back with me. He's really angry. He killed a chicken specially."

"Oh," Nina says, sheepishly. "OK. I'd better tell Helmut. Come with me."

I follow Nina through the chateau, making a map in my mind. We stop in the kitchen. There's a big pot of stew on the stove. It smells wonderful. Nina gets out a smaller pot. "Fill that. We'll take it for you and Dad to eat. I'll cook the chicken tomorrow."

I'm not sure that Uncle will accept German food, but now isn't the time to tell Nina that. "I'm on the bike," I say. "You'll have to carry it."

That doesn't please Nina either. Two minutes later, she's back. Helmut's with her.

"Come on," he says. "I'll drive you down to the farm. We can put the bike in the back of the jeep."

And that's what we do, the three of us cramming into the front of the jeep. Helmut chats cheerfully in French.

"There'll be more people in Villefranche soon. We've started evacuating coastal areas."

"Why?" I ask.

"Getting ready for the Allied invasion."

"Do you think it'll all be over soon?"

Helmut nods. "A few more months, that's all."

"You sound like you're happy to lose," I comment.

"I'll be happy when it's over, win or lose. Won't you?"

I admit that I will. All I really want is to go back to Paris, to be with Mum and Dad again.

We stop at the road to the farm. Nina and I walk along the the road, me wheeling a bike, her holding a heavy pot.

"What will Helmut do back in Germany?" I ask.

"Teach at Leipzig University. Imagine, one day, I'll be a professor's wife, living in Germany!"

I try to imagine this, but fail. Uncle Henri's pleased to see us. I'd worried that he wouldn't eat the Germans' food, but he scoffs it down. Me too. Afterwards, though, I get stomach ache, from eating too much rich food too quickly. But it's not that which keeps me awake. It's the thought of all that coal, and Philippe, out there in the cold.

In Paris, I got irritated when people talked about waiting for *the right moment* to resist the Germans. I thought that waiting was an excuse. Now, though, I remember what Mum said to me just before I left Paris. *Sometimes it's brave to be a coward and cowardly to be brave.* Is Philippe being brave, hiding in the woods? I can't decide. Is this the right moment to help him?

10 ✳ The Maquis Camp

On Monday morning, I tell Uncle Henri I'm going to fix fences. Instead, I head for the woods. I don't know exactly where the local Maquis camp is, but I have a rough idea. With no leaves on the trees, they shouldn't be too difficult to find. And I have a compass with me, just in case I get lost.

Five kilometres from home, on the edge of the mountains, I see wisps of wood smoke. I head in that direction.

I don't know what I expect to find. A ragamuffin army, maybe, sat around a camp-fire, wearing animal pelts, with guns by their side. They'll have an armed guard, probably, but no one would mistake me for a German, or a Miliciand. I'm too small, too young-looking. Even so, I'm scared.

I get nearer to the smoke. My every step makes a crunching noise in the brittle, frozen earth. No one challenges me. The spindly branches of the silver birch trees remind me of skeletons. Through them I can see a clearing. Something's moving.

"Friend coming!" I call out, as I walk towards them. I hope it is them. One thing worries me. If it is the Maquis, and I can find them so easily, then so can the Milice.

Suddenly, a wiry figure jumps from behind the trees. He wears a fur hat and a ragged overcoat. He's pointing a rifle at me.

"Hello again, Georges," I say.

"Come to join us?" Georges says. "You're too skinny. You'd never make it out here in the cold."

"I'm not staying. I've got some information."

Georges leads me to the ragged camp. Four men sit around a puny fire. None of them is Philippe.

"Want a look around?" Georges asks.

"Sure."

He shows me the caves where they bed down. "When the ground's not iced over," he says, "we make dug-outs. They're more secure."

There's also an old Army tent which can be taken down quickly. They've moved twice so far, Georges says.

"The Milice don't get near us."

"How come?"

"We have a spy in the local Milice. We know what they're going to do before they do!"

He shouldn't be telling me this, I think.

"Don't you have a lorry?" I ask.

"It belongs to a farmer who supports us. There's a road on the other side of the mountains, about half an hour's walk away. The lorry's in a barn near there. Why do you want to know?"

"You'll need one after you've heard what I've got to say."

Philippe returns, carrying more wood for the fire. "So, you finally decided which side you're on, eh, Jean?"

"Sort of," I say. "I've got a way for you to be warmer." I tell them everything I saw at the chateau. Georges isn't too impressed by the coal.

"Coal's heavy to transport and gives out more smoke than wood. We'll take some, but to give away, not for using here. I'm interested in this radio room. Could you show us where it is?"

"I'm not going back there," I tell him. "I'd be recognised."

"Not if we went at night," Georges says.

"I'll think about it," I say, as Philippe puts broken branches onto the fire. "Is this all of you there is?"

"This week, yes," Georges says. "But there are many more men we can call on if we have an operation to carry out."

"How many of you were at Oyonnax last month?" I ask.

Georges laughs. "None from Villefranche. That was a top secret operation. Why do you think...?" He sees me looking at Philippe, who is staring at the fire. "Making up stories again, were you, Philippe?"

"I didn't really believe him," I tell Georges, though I had, completely. I realise that Philippe's story about sabotaging the railway line was made up, too. He probably waited until it was over, then went to look.

"It was a famous victory," Georges tells me. "Is that what brought you here, wanting to be part of another one?"

"No, I..." I was worried about them being cold, but that sounds like a wimpy thing to say. "I only wanted to help."

"Good. What were you doing up at the German garrison, anyway?"

"It's hardly a garrison," I say. "I was looking for..." I see Philippe's expression. He's glaring at me. I realise the others don't know that his sister works for the Germans.

"I was taking a message," I say. Then I look at the setting sun. "It's late. My uncle thinks I'm working. I'd better go."

"We'll call on you soon," Georges says. "Thanks for the information."

I shouldn't have gone, I decide, as I walk home. For what if Nina's there when the Maquis raid the chateau? She might recognise some of them. And worse, they might recognise her.

11 ✳ The Raid

Should I warn Nina about the Maquis raid? She's usually home just after dark, but sometimes she stays late. The raid is bound to happen after dark, but it gets dark early these days.

"I looked for you a while back," Uncle Henri says, "but didn't find you."

I hesitate. My uncle's been so good to me, I can't tell him a direct lie.

"I went to see Philippe," I say.

My uncle raises an eyebrow, but doesn't say anything about the fib I told earlier.

"How is he?"

"All right, I think. Cold. Most of the Maquis seem to be living at home at the moment."

"Yes, I expect he'll be back again before long," Uncle says. "Did he have any more tall stories for you?"

"Tall stories?"

"Like the one he told about being on parade at Oyonnax."

"You knew that wasn't true?"

Uncle Henri smiles. "Philippe has a vivid imagination. He likes to play at being an outlaw in the woods. But it's only a game, Jean. Don't let him draw you into it."

"But he's on the right side!" I say.

Uncle Henri shrugs his shoulders. "The Germans will be gone soon. That's thanks to the Allies, not thanks to the Maquis. Keep that in mind and don't do anything stupid."

It's good advice, but it comes too late.

* * * * *

A few days later, close to midnight, Philippe sneaks into the house to get me.

"We're going to the chateau," he says, once he's woken me up. "We need you with us."

"Why?" I ask, sleepily.

"You've been inside. You know your way around."

So does Nina, I think, but he isn't asking her. I protest.

"I told you where..."

"Come on, Jean. The lorry's at the end of the road."

Still only half awake, I dress quickly and

quietly. At least Nina's home. The Maquis won't find out that she works in the chateau. I hurry out to the lorry. There are six men sitting in the back. I don't recognise any of them. In the front, Georges is driving. Philippe explains the plan.

"We chose tonight because men from the garrison were seen drinking in Villefranche, celebrating somebody's birthday. So they'll sleep heavily. We'll go for the coal first. Once we've loaded up, we'll try and get into the radio room."

"You'd better be right about how few Germans there are guarding the place," Georges says. "Here, put this on."

It's a woollen hat which can be pulled down to cover the face. Holes have been cut out for the eyes.

We drive slowly, with no lights on.

"How come you got sent to the chateau?" Georges wants to know. "Friendly with the Germans, are you?"

"Hardly."

"What was the message you were sent with?" Georges asks.

"Let him be," Philippe tells Georges. "If a German tells him to deliver a message, he has to do it. And he can't read German. Can you, Jean?"

"No, I can't," I say, then call out. "Careful!"

Georges almost steers into the ditch. Now he goes even more slowly. At the chateau, a single light burns. The night is overcast, moonless. A good night for thieves.

"Leave the road over there." I point to the right of the chateau. "It's safer than the drive. The ground's pretty flat."

"Is there space to turn around?" Georges asks. "The reverse gear on this lorry is terrible."

"As long as you don't get too close." The lorry clatters and groans as we go onto the grass. I'm sure we'll be heard, but nobody comes. We stop behind an outhouse. I point out where the coal is stored. Georges turns the lorry around so that it's faced in the right direction for a getaway. Then we lower the ramp at the back of the lorry. One of the Maquisards brings down a wheelbarrow.

"This is good," Philippe says. "See? We needed you here."

At Philippe's suggestion, I keep watch. I'm at one end of the chateau. He's at the other. Loading the lorry takes ages. We make so much noise that I'm sure we'll be heard. In a shooting match, we'd have no chance. Only Philippe and Georges have guns. I can't see where Georges has gone.

Then, suddenly, Georges reappears. They've got enough coal now. Georges signals Philippe and me over to him. "All right. Let's go in."

"Maybe it's too big a risk," Philippe says. "If they come after us, their jeeps are bound to overtake the lorry."

"We know the roads better than they do," Georges tells him. "And I've just slashed the tyres on both of their jeeps. I've checked the door. Two of us should be able to kick it in."

He and Philippe go at the door. It's noisy. Even with two of them, it takes a full minute to break. They're bound to have woken everybody in the house. Masks pulled down over our heads, we charge into the dusty hall. For a moment, it's unfamiliar. Philippe has a lantern which he waves around.

"Fourth door on the left," I say. I don't want to go in with them. They're bigger and better at smashing things up than I am.

"Here." Philippe hands me his revolver. "Cover us."

They go. I shiver. I've never held a gun before. I don't like it. I don't even know if the safety catch is on or not. My hand trembles so much that I worry I may fire the gun by accident.

The radio room is unlocked, as it was before. I hear the two of them doing damage. Crashing noises echo down the corridor. Someone is bound to come. But there's no light, and I won't be able to hear anything because of the noise from the radio room. What am I doing here? I must be mad.

I hear more laughter, crashing noises. They're taking too long. My eyes are getting used to the darkness. There's nobody in the corridor to my left, but I see a shadow in the corridor to my right. I step back, holding the pistol high. Behind me, I hear Georges and Philippe coming out. They're carrying the lantern. Now I can see more than a shadow.

Standing in the corridor to my right is a man. It's Helmut. He's holding a rifle, but it's not pointed, whereas my gun is.

"Come on, Jean!" Philippe says. He hasn't seen Helmut.

I groan. Helmut has heard my name. I hesitate. Because of the light from the lantern, I can no longer see Helmut.

"Come on!" I follow Georges and Philippe

out of the chateau, into the lorry. Nobody comes after us. We drive over the fields onto the road, back towards the hideout. Helmut could have shot us, but he didn't. Why? Because we might have shot back, and he's a coward? Or because he worked out who I was?

"Let me out," I tell Georges as we pass my uncle's farm.

"You can't go," Georges tells me. "You're one of us now."

"Let him leave," Philippe says.

"Maybe you want to go home, too, Philippe," Georges teases.

"My home is Paris, not here," I point out.

Georges slams on the brakes. "Go on, then, if you must. Quickly." I go.

I sneak into the house and go to bed. I'm scared for myself, and scared for Nina. Will she be blamed for the raid? Helmut heard my name. If he makes the connection, we could both be executed.

Was this the right moment to fight back? I'm not sure. Maybe the right moment was back in 1940, when the Germans invaded Paris and half the city ran away. Why resist now, when the war is nearly over? By this time tomorrow, I may be dead. And for what? A few lumps of coal and a broken radio.

12 ✳ Jour-J

Every day, for days, I wait for the Germans to come for me. They don't. Helmut heard my name, but 'Jean' is a very common name. Maybe he thought nothing of it. Nina doesn't even mention the attack on the radio room.

A few weeks later, the Milice sweep through the woods near the mountains. They find the Maquis camp, but it's abandoned. The Maquis are everywhere now. Nobody knows which are real Maquis and which are bandits, pretending. All over the country, there are raids, acts of sabotage, even bank robberies. General de Gaulle, leader of the Free French, speaks on the BBC. He says that the Maquis should only engage in sabotage. Only he doesn't call them the Maquis any more. The resisters who obey de Gaulle are now the FFI, the Forces Françaises Intérieur. 'Maquis' has become a dirty word.

De Gaulle's words are ignored. Raids continue.

One day, out of the blue, Philippe turns up. When I get in from the fields, he's in the parlour, taking a bath. His body is painfully thin.

"Where's Nina?" he asks.

"At the chateau, as usual."

"She ought to quit," he says.

"They wouldn't let her."

"German control is breaking down. They've only got a little time left. She doesn't want to get caught in the middle."

"I'll tell her," I say, then I change the subject, mentioning what I've heard on the radio.

"De Gaulle doesn't want us to do anything which will provoke reprisals," Philippe explains. "The Germans have been known to shoot innocent people when they can't find us."

"Did they get close to you in the woods?" I ask.

"Nowhere near," Philippe says, then laughs. "Want to hear a story? We were hiding out in the woods and these men appeared. Some were dressed like Milice, so we got ready to fight back. Then they saw us. Guns were raised. We were about to start a shoot–out when I recognised one of them. Paul Lurcat!"

That was Paul, the cattle driver, the tobacco

smuggler.

"I knew it was him from the way he held his stick! I thought for a moment that he'd joined the Milice. So I called his name and asked his business. 'If you can't beat 'em, join em' he said. Seems that he'd joined this gang who call themselves a Maquis unit. Really, they're a bunch of thieves, a faux Maquis. But they find it's safest to disguise themselves as Milice."

"That's ridiculous," I say.

"The Maquis often disguise themselves as Milice," Philippe tells me. "It keeps the enemy confused. Now, remember what I said. The war will be over soon. Tell Nina to quit working for the Germans, or people will hold it against her."

* * * * *

That night, when Nina returns from work, it's late. I'm ready for sleep, but go to her room. I tell her what Philippe said.

"I won't quit," Nina replies. "I'm going to leave with Helmut when the war ends."

"Suppose Helmut doesn't get away?" I suggest, gently.

"Why would anyone punish Helmut?" Nina snaps at me. "He's not hurt anybody. Even when the Maquis smashed up the radio room, there were no reprisals. If that had happened at other garrisons, the Germans would have picked people from the village at random and shot them. Helmut didn't even pick you up."

"Me?" I ask.

"Some idiot called out your name, remember?"

Embarrassed, I stutter, "Jean's a common name."

"True, but there can't be many men in the Maquis as small as you, Jean. I suppose Philippe was with you? No. Don't answer that. And don't worry about me. I can look after myself."

* * * * *

Everyone you meet is talking about Jour-J, which the British call D-Day. That's when the Allies will invade France. But nobody knows when it is.

Then, suddenly, in June, when we're getting the hay in, it happens. The invasion is far away, on the other side of the country, but it gives heart to the Maquis. Philippe shows up soon after, looking for Nina.

"Where is she? Didn't you give her my

message?"

"I did. Are the Maquis about to take over round here?"

"No. In some towns, the Maquis took over after they thought the Nazis were gone. Only then the Nazis came back, started shooting everyone. So we have to be careful. But it won't be long now. Tell Nina she must stop working at the chateau."

That night, I tell Nina what Philippe said.

"He's right," she answers. "It's nearly over. Helmut's waiting for instructions to leave. But it's difficult. Lots of the country is in the hands of the Maquis. The Germans need to choose their time and their escape route carefully."

"Will Helmut take you with him when he goes?" I ask.

"Of course he will," she says, in a frightened voice. "Or if he can't, he'll make arrangements for me to join him later."

But next day, when she gets to work, the Germans are gone.

13 ✳ Liberation

I'm working in the fields when Nina comes with the news.

"He's gone without me, Jean. How could he do that?"

All over France, the Germans are sneaking away in the night. Why should Helmut be any different?

"He probably had no choice, Nina. You ought to go into the village, tell people they've gone. That way, you'll be the bearer of good news. People will forget you worked for them."

"That's a good idea," Nina says, through her tears. After she's cleaned herself up, we walk to the village together. There's movement up at the chateau. A lorry is parked outside the gates.

"Are you sure they've gone?" I ask Nina, remembering what Philippe told me about Germans seeming to leave, then returning.

"They're long gone," Nina replies.

"I can see a lorry up there." I recognise the lorry. It's Paul Lurcat's, the one that was stolen.

I'll bet he got it back when he joined the faux Maquis.

"They're probably looting the chateau," Nina says.

"Have the Germans left much behind? " I ask.

"No, but there's a lot of stuff belonging to the French family who own the place."

We reach the village. Nina announces the good news in the Mairie and the bakery, telling everyone who'll listen. People hug in the marketplace. Bottles of wine appear. I want to celebrate, too, but I'm scared for Nina.

Proudly, the Villefranche Maquis march into the market place. Georges and Philippe wave French flags. A few minutes later, they're followed by the lorry with the faux Maquis which Paul belongs to. This lot are already drunk on looted wine.

"Where is she?" Paul shouts. "Find the German-lover!"

I realise who he means before Nina does. Of course, Paul knows that Nina worked at the chateau.

"You're drunk!" Philippe says. "Don't insult my sister!"

"Don't tell me you didn't know about her," Paul taunts.

"She worked as a maid for the Germans. So what?"

"A maid? Your sister's a..." Paul says a dirty word. Philippe tries to hit him. Paul ducks, then sneers. "Want proof? Here, I found this in the chateau!"

"So they made me work in the chateau," Nina calls out, and the crowd can see where she is. "So what?"

Then Nina sees what Paul is holding. She tries to run but people block her way. She's surrounded.

On the cobbled ground, I find what Paul Lurcat was holding. It's a photograph of Helmut and Nina, their arms around each other, smiling. Helmut, her lover, must have left it behind, like he left Nina behind. I watch as the crowd drags my cousin away. Philippe comes over to me, looks at the photo.

"Did you know?" he asks me.

Shamefaced, I nod.

"Come on," my cousin says, his face white with anger. "They might want you next. I'll take you home, where it's safe."

"What happened?" Uncle Henri asks, back at the farm. "Paul came charging in here like a mad bull, looking for Nina."

Philippe tells him.

"I should never have let her work there," Uncle says.

Philippe doesn't answer this. "I only came back because I wanted Jean out of the way," he says. "Now I'm going back for Nina."

* * * * *

It's dark when my two cousins return. If I didn't know that one of them was Nina, I wouldn't recognise her. Her clothes are filthy. Her body is covered in bruises. Her front teeth are missing.

And her long, beautiful hair is gone. Nina's shaved head is covered in cuts. I can't stop myself from crying. Nina's face stays dry. I reach out to squeeze her hand. She flinches, like we're strangers.

"I thought they'd kill me," she says, still trembling. "They shaved Marie Caziot's head and all she did was smile at the Germans she served in the shop. They were mad, crazy."

Suddenly, she bursts into tears. "Oh, Helmut, Helmut..."

My uncle slaps her across the face. "I never want to hear that name again."

14 ✳ The Right Moment

A week later, the radio tells us that the Germans have left Paris. I try to persuade Nina to go home with me. There's no future for her here, I argue. But Nina won't come. Her hair marks her out, she says. People will know.

She's right. When I get back to Paris, there are stories of women who've been hung for going with Germans. Everyone blames everyone else for letting the Germans walk all over us. All sorts of people are attacked. The only ones who don't seem to get punished are those like Paul Lurcat. Food is still scarce and everyone needs to use the black market.

* * * * *

A few months later, Nina does come to Paris. Her hair has grown. Her teeth are fixed. She's almost beautiful, but not quite. She will never be beautiful again.

"You were right," she tells me. "I couldn't

stay in Villefranche. People spit at me when I walk by on the street. Old friends ignore me."

"You'll be all right here," my mother says. That night, we make her up a bed in our tiny kitchen. Next day, Mum gets Nina a job in the laundry.

* * * * *

They're both at work in spring, 1945, when there's a knock on the door. I'm just back from school and hurry to open it. I always hurry, waiting for a moment which one day must surely come.

On the landing there's a thin, tired-looking man in an old French Army uniform. I hardly recognise him. He hardly recognises me.

"Dad?" I say.

"Jean?" Awkwardly, my father reaches out for me.

The war is really over.

Further Reading and Acknowledgements

I found *Paris in the Third Reich* (Collins, 1981) by David Pryce-Jones very useful when writing the Paris section of the story. H.R.Kedward's *In Search of the Maquis: Rural Resistance in Southern France 1942-44* (Clarendon Press, 1993) helped with the background in the South, as did (via e-mail) my friend, Jan Dodd, in Gascony.

I am most indebted to Ian Ousby's gripping, comprehensive *Occupation: The Ordeal of France 1940-44* (John Murray, 1997), which inspired me to write this book in the first place. I hope that I was able to keep in mind something that Ousby writes in his preface: "Those who look at how people in another time and another country behaved in an hour of darkness find no easy clue as to how they themselves might behave should they suffer a similar ordeal."